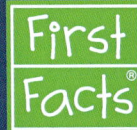

First Facts
U.S. NATIONAL PARKS FIELD GUIDES

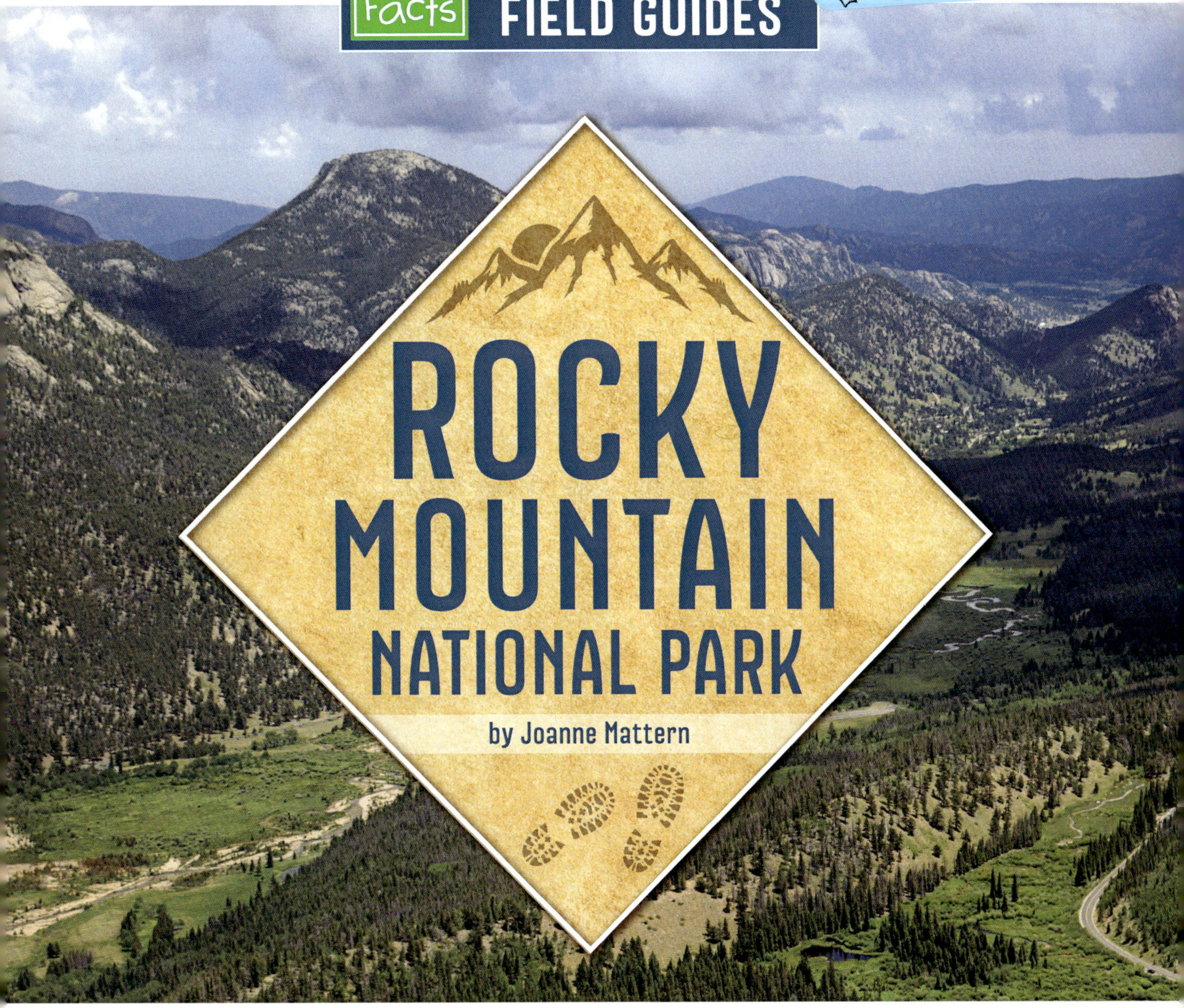

ROCKY MOUNTAIN NATIONAL PARK

by Joanne Mattern

PEBBLE
a capstone imprint

First Facts Books are published by Pebble,
1710 Roe Crest Drive, North Mankato, Minnesota 56003
www.mycapstone.com

Copyright © 2019 by Pebble, a Capstone imprint. All rights reserved. No part of this publication may be reproduced in whole or in part, or stored in a retrieval system, or transmitted in any form or by any means, electronic, mechanical, photocopying, recording, or otherwise, without written permission of the publisher.

Library of Congress Cataloging-in-Publication Data is available on the Library of Congress website.
ISBN 978-1-9771-0355-0 (library binding)
ISBN 978-1-9771-0525-7 (paperback)
ISBN 978-1-9771-0362-8 (ebook pdf)

Editorial Credits:
Anna Butzer, editor
Juliette Peters, designer
Tracy Cummins, media researcher
Kathy McColley, production specialist

Photo Credits:
Capstone: Eric Gohl, 9 Bottom, 15 Top, 19; iStockphoto: milehightraveler, 11 Bottom Right, NNehring, 16 Bottom, RiverNorthPhotography, 11 Top; Minden Pictures: Tim Fitzharris, 8–9; Shutterstock: Alexey Kamenskiy, 7, Alfie Photography, 3 Top, Arne Beruldsen, 14–15, bjul, 2–3, 22–23, 24, Cat_arch_angel, Design Element, Christine Krahl, Design Element, Christopher Jackson, Back Cover, Cover Top, Colin S. Osburn, 3 Bottom, Danita Delmont, 3 Middle, Eivor Kuchta, 13 Middle, Gloria V Moeller, 11 Bottom Left, Gray Photo Online, Cover Bottom Middle, haveseen, 18, Jason Patrick Ross, 16 Middle, KanokpolTokumhnerd, Design Element, Kelly vanDellen, 15 Bottom, Kerry Hargrove, 13 Bottom, Magda van der Kleij, 8 Right, Nelson Sirlin, 4–5, Rick Fansler, 8 Left, RIRF Stock, 17, rsinclair71, 16 Top, Ryan DeBerardinis, Cover Bottom Left, Sputnik Aloysius, 12, Steve Boice, 5 Bottom, Steve Bower, 6–7, Steven Schremp, Cover Bottom Right, 20 Bottom, 20–21, viewgene, Design Element, Vlad Klok, Design Element, Wendy Ringel, 10–11, Yobab, 1, 13 Top

Printed and bound in the USA.
1335

Table of Contents

Welcome to Rocky Mountain
    National Park................4
Up the Mountains................6
The Rocky Mountain Tundra.......10
Nature's Waterpark..............14
Hiking Through History..........18

    Glossary........................22
    Read More.......................23
    Internet Sites..................23
    Critical Thinking Questions.....24
    Index...........................24

Welome to Rocky Mountain National Park

Where can you find 77 mountain peaks taller than 12,000 feet (3,657 meters)? Visit Rocky Mountain National Park. It is one of the highest national parks in the United States. Many visitors say it feels like being on top of the world.

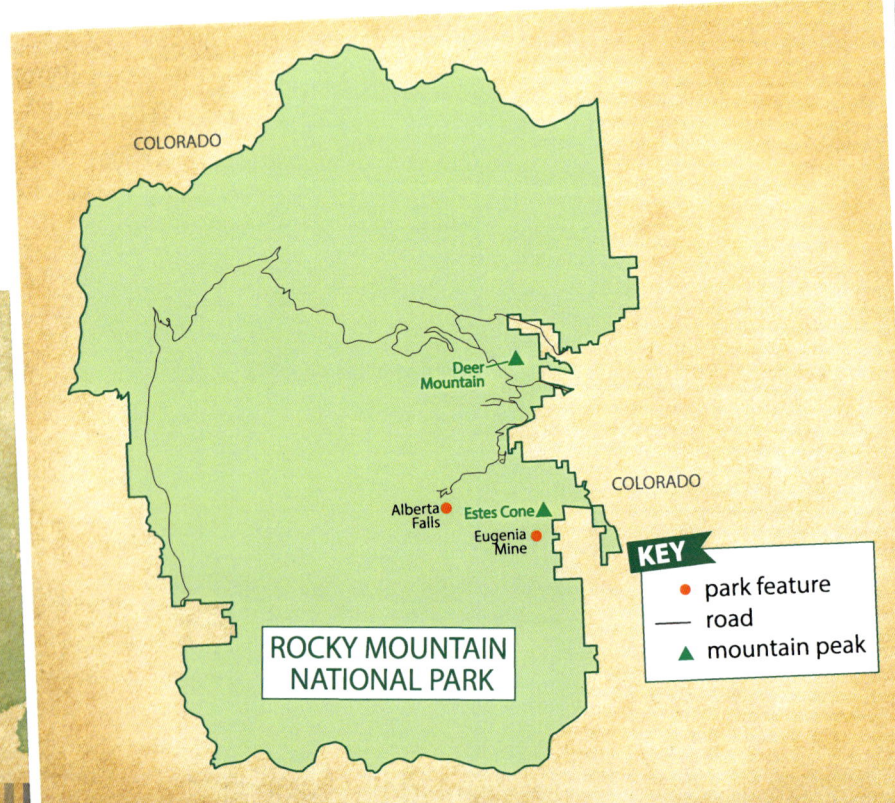

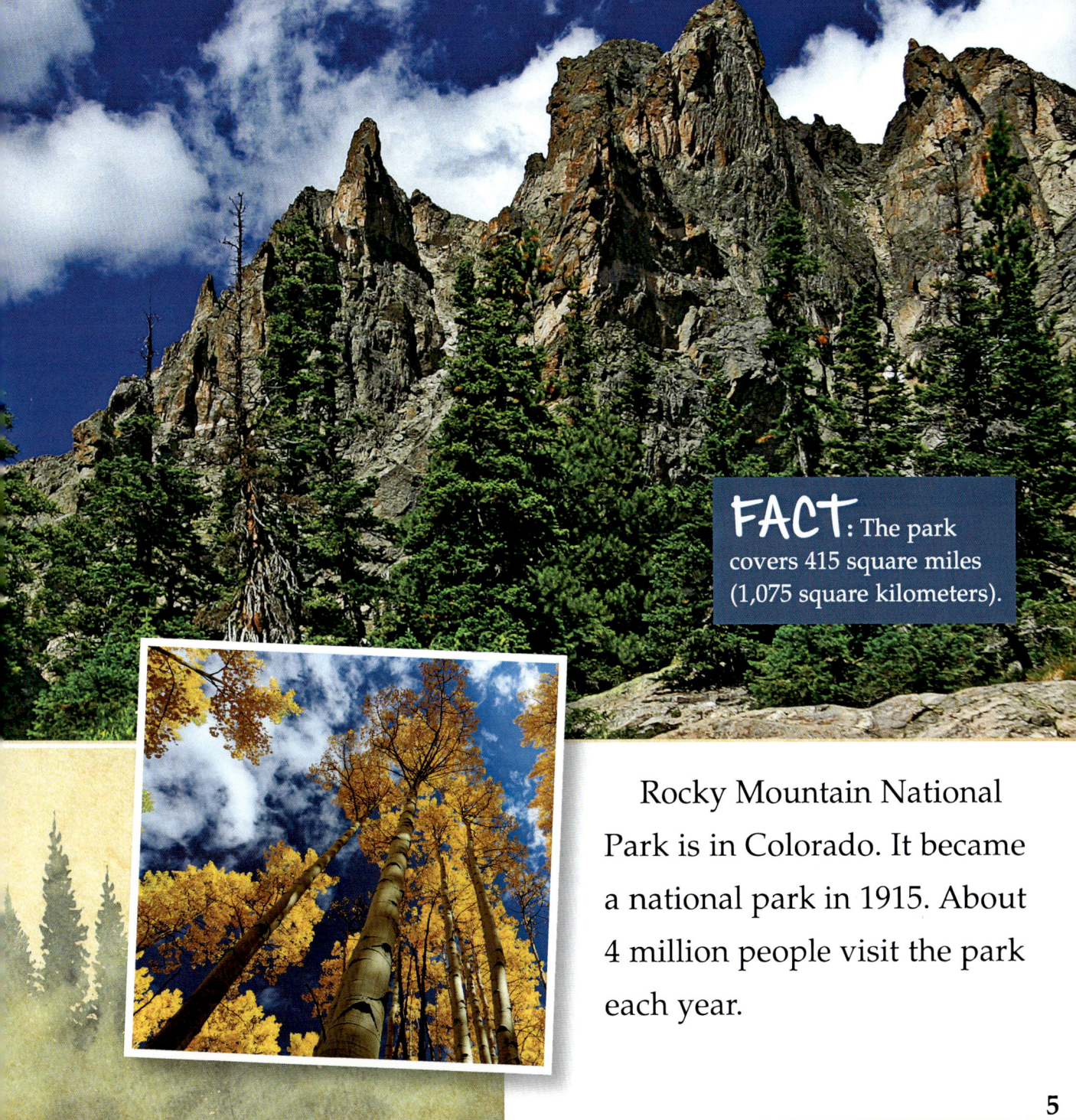

FACT: The park covers 415 square miles (1,075 square kilometers).

Rocky Mountain National Park is in Colorado. It became a national park in 1915. About 4 million people visit the park each year.

5

Up the Mountains

The Rocky Mountains formed millions of years ago. **Tectonic plates** under the earth's crust pushed rocks up to make mountains. Water and wind shaped the mountains through **erosion**.

tectonic plate—a gigantic slab of Earth's crust that moves around on magma

erosion—wearing away of rock or soil by wind, water, or ice

Then **glaciers** passed through. They moved rocks and shaped **valleys**. Glaciers made the land in the Rocky Mountain National Park into how it looks today.

glacier—huge masses of ice that move slowly across land

valley—an area of low ground between two hills, usually containing a river

The park has more than 350 miles (563 km) of hiking trails. Deer Mountain Trail is one of the most popular. It starts in a forest. The trail then passes through valleys. Visitors often see elk or bison here. Finally, the trail climbs Deer Mountain. This mountain is about 10,000 feet (3,048 m) high. Hike to the top and have a picnic while looking at the amazing views.

^ bison

< elk

The Rocky Mountain Tundra

Rocky Mountain National Park has a **tundra** climate in some areas. The tundra climate is only found at high **altitudes**. It is cold and windy. Plants and mosses grow close to the ground here. There are small, bright flowers. But there are no trees.

Protect the Tundra
Stay on Paved Trail

^ elephant head flower

butterflies ^

tundra—flat land where the ground under the soil is always frozen

altitude—how high a place is above sea level or Earth's surface

11

^ Tundra Communities Trail

To visit the tundra, visitors walk the Tundra Communities Trail. This trail is only 1 mile long (1.6 km). But it can be a difficult hike. The air is thin because the trail is so high. It can be hard for people to breathe.

FACT: It can snow any day of the year on this trail, even in the summer.

On this short trail, hikers might see furry animals like **pikas** or **marmots**. They might see ground birds like the ptarmigan. Or hawks might fly over their heads.

pika—small mammal related to rabbits
marmot—rodent that lives underground in the mountains

marmot >

^ pika

< ptarmigan

Nature's Waterpark

The park features more than mountains. There are 156 lakes and 31 waterfalls. Visitors hike the Alberta Falls Trail. This path passes many waterfalls on the way to Alberta Falls. There, water rushes 30 feet (9 m) down into Glacier Creek. It is a noisy, splashy place.

KEY
- Alberta Falls Trail
- park feature
- trail
- road
- river

Alberta Falls Trail

FACT: Alberta Falls is named after Alberta Sprague. She and her family were some of the first people to live in the area in the 1870s.

15

Many animals live in the park's lakes and streams. Beavers build their homes in ponds and lakes. The lakes are full of fish too. Birds make nests along the shore. Small **amphibians**, such as boreal toads and wood frogs also live by the lakes. Insects fly over the water.

beaver

black-billed magpie

boreal toad

amphibian—a cold-blooded animal with a backbone; amphibians live in water when young and can live on land as adults

FACT: Moose are the largest animal that live in Rocky Mountain National Park.

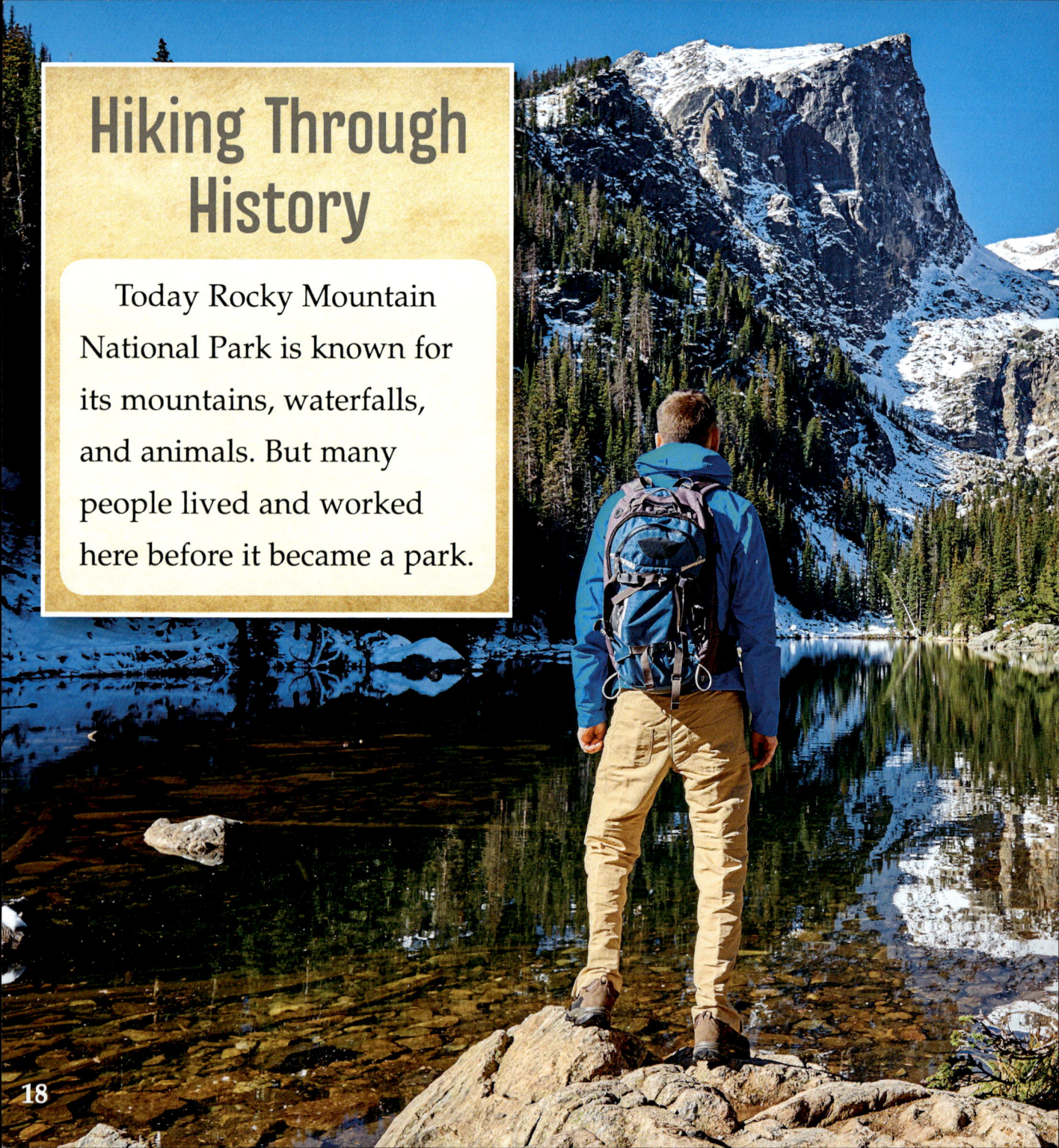

Hiking Through History

Today Rocky Mountain National Park is known for its mountains, waterfalls, and animals. But many people lived and worked here before it became a park.

More than 100 years ago, people mined for **minerals** in the mountains. In 1905 the Eugenia Mine opened. Workers carried copper and gold out of the mountains using carts pulled by horses.

mineral—a material found in nature that is not an animal or a plant

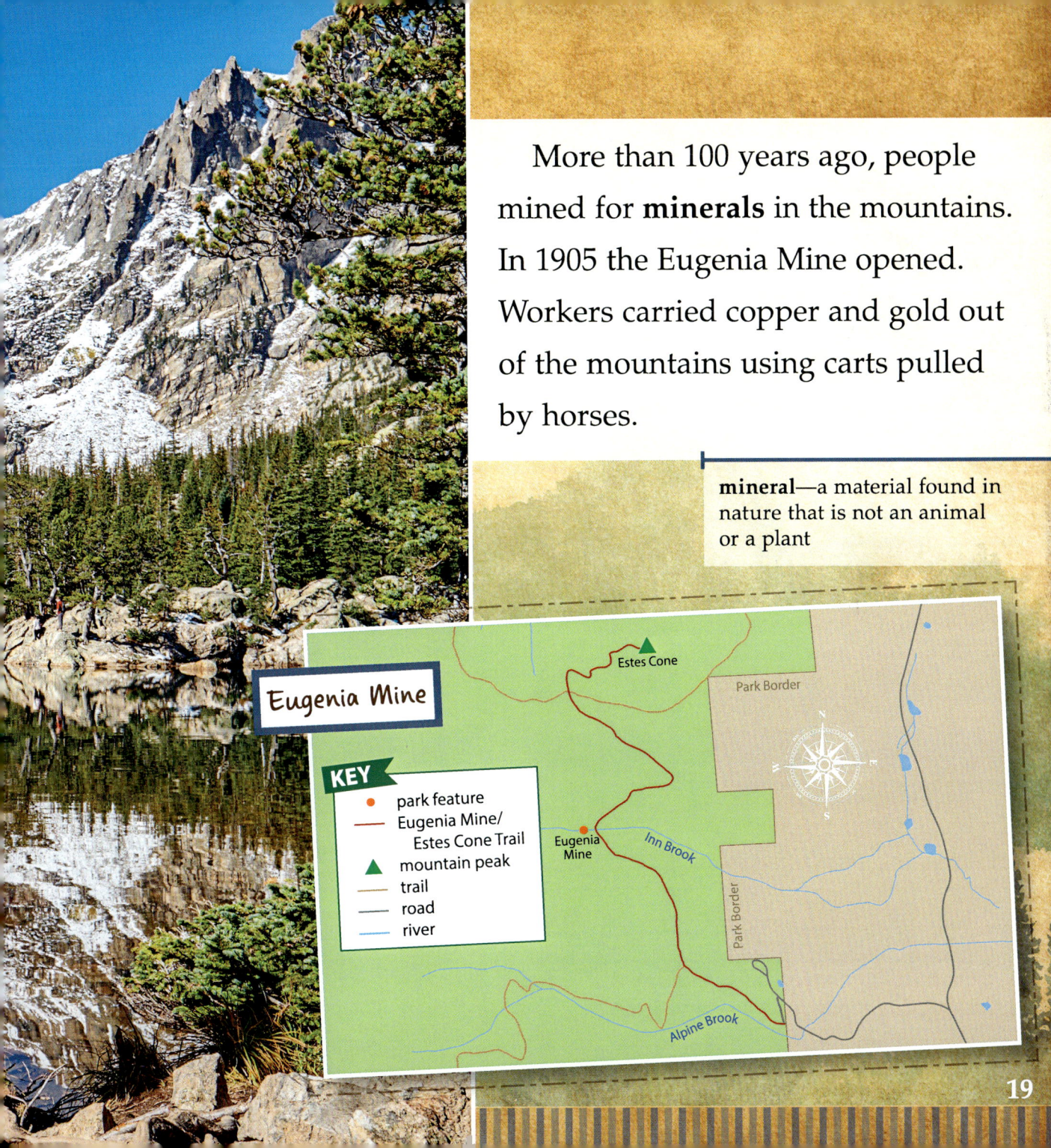

Eugenia Mine

KEY
- park feature
- Eugenia Mine/ Estes Cone Trail
- mountain peak
- trail
- road
- river

19

< Estes Cone

^ view from top of Estes Cone

The Eugenia Mine Trail leads visitors through the woods where the mine used to be. Visitors can continue on Estes Cone Trail for 1.6 miles (2.6 km) to the Estes Cone peak. This spot gives visitors amazing views of this beautiful national park.

Glossary

altitude (AL-ti-tood)—how high a place is above sea level or Earth's surface

amphibian (am-FI-bee-uhn)—a cold-blooded animal with a backbone; amphibians live in water when young and can live on land as adults

erosion (i-ROH-zhuhn)—wearing away of rock by water and wind

glacier (GLAY-shur)—huge masses of ice that move slowly across land

marmot (MAR-met)—rodent that lives underground in the mountains

mineral (MIN-ur-uhl)—a material found in nature that is not an animal or a plant

pika (PEYE-kuh)—small mammals related to rabbits

tectonic plate (tek-TON-ik PLAYTE)—giant slab of Earth's crust that moves around on magma

tundra (TUHN-druh)—flat land where the ground under the soil is always frozen

valley (VAL-ee)—an area of land between hills, usually containing a river

Read More

Aloian, Molly. *The Rocky Mountains National Park.* Mountains Around the World. New York: Crabtree Publishing Company, 2012.

Herrington, Lisa. *Rocky Mountain National Park.* Rookie National Parks. New York: Children's Press, 2018.

Zeiger, Jennifer. *Rocky Mountain.* National Parks. New York: Children's Press, 2018.

Internet Sites

Use FactHound to find Internet sites related to this book:

Visit *www.facthound.com*

Just type in 9781977103550 and go.

 Check out projects, games and lots more at *www.capstonekids.com*

Critical Thinking Questions

1. Describe some of the animals that live in Rocky Mountain National Park. Which one would you like to learn more about?

2. What part of Rocky Mountain National Park would you most like to visit? Why?

3. Part of Rocky Mountain National Park has a tundra climate. Describe the tundra and the plants and animals living there.

Index

Alberta Falls, 14, 15
animals, 8, 13, 16, 17, 18, 19

Deer Mountain, 8

erosion, 6
Estes Cone, 21
Eugenia Mine, 19, 21

forests, 8
formation, 6

glaciers, 7

history, 5, 18–19

location, 5

mountains, 4, 6, 8, 14, 18, 19

plants, 10

size, 5

trails, 8, 12, 13, 14, 21
tundra, 10, 12

valleys, 7, 8

water features, 6, 14, 16, 18

24